The Big Race
A lesson on perseverance

by Suzanne I. Barchers
illustrated by Mattia Cerato

RED
CHAIR
•PRESS•

Please visit our website at **www.redchairpress.com**.
Find a free catalog of all our high-quality products for young readers.

The Big Race
Library of Congress Control Number: 2012931799
ISBN: 978-1-937529-16-1 (pbk)
ISBN: 978-1-937529-24-6 (hc)

Lexile is a registered trademark of MetaMetrics, Inc. Used with permission.
Leveling provided by Linda Cornwell of Literacy Connections Consulting.

This edition first published in 2012 by
Red Chair Press, LLC   PO Box 333   South Egremont, MA 01258-0333

Printed in China
1 2 3 4 5 16 15 14 13 12

Bun

Pip

Sox

Tab

Ted

The Big Race

Sox can't wait for the day of the big race! Sox is a fast runner and hopes to win. But when the usually lazy Tab decides to train for the race too, Tab asks Sox to help. Can Sox help Tab get ready for the race and still run to win?

"Let's go!" Sox says, as he ties his shoelace.
"Let's go sign up for next Saturday's race!"

4

"Go ahead, Sox," Ted says with a yawn.
"I don't like to race. But I'll cheer you on."

Later, Sox dreams about winning the race.
Then Sox sees Tab. There's a smile on Tab's face.

6

"Hi, Tab!" says Sox. "Where have you been?"
"I signed up for the race," Tab says with a grin.

"I know I'm not fast. This will be my first race.
But I'm really steady. I'll keep a good pace.

Would you help me train, Sox? You run so fast. Perhaps I could win a blue ribbon at last."

Sox stops in confusion. He can't think what to say.
He knows he runs faster than Tab any day.

Then Sox says to Tab, "I'll help all I can.
Let's meet in the morning. We'll make a plan."

The next day they meet and go for a run.
They go just one block. Tab says, "This is fun.

I think I like running. But it's hot in the sun.
How far should we go before we are done?"

Tab trudges along for two blocks, then three.
Sox stops and says, "Tab, let's rest by that tree.

We'll run more tomorrow. We're just beginning.
Don't give up yet. Just think about winning."

The next day Tab tries hard to pick up the pace.
He gasps as he asks, "Could I win first place?"

"You might," Sox replies. "I really don't know.
You're getting faster." But Sox knows Tab is slow.

The friends keep training more every day.
Tab hopes he'll be ready to win on race day.

Sox does not know just what he will do.
He can run faster. And Sox wants to win too.

On race day, Sox says, "Do you see who's here?"
"Hurray Sox and Tab!" their friends yell and cheer.

Then the race starts. They dash up the street.
The training has helped. Tab's fast on his feet.

But Sox falls to his knee. He's tripped on a lace.
"Don't stop, Tab," he shouts. "Go win the race!"

"I can't leave you, Sox. You've hurt your knee.
Without you along, what fun would it be?"

With Tab helping Sox, they finish the race.
Their friends cheer them on as they come in last place.

24

Sox says to Tab, "Getting hurt isn't fun.
But with you by my side, I feel like we won!"

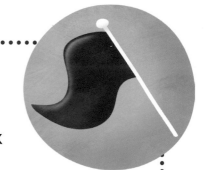

Big Questions:

Why do you think Tab asked Sox to help train for the race? Was Tab ready when the race began?

Do you think Tab and Sox were sad to finish in last place? How do you think they feel?

Big Words:

confusion: to not understand something

pace: the speed at which something happens

train: to teach a skill through practice

Has a friend or younger brother or sister ever asked you for help with something you were good at? Does it make you feel good to help or does it bother you to be asked?

Think about something you want to learn to do. Who could you ask to teach you? Do you think they would like to help out?

Activity

Sox was a fast runner. Tab wanted to learn to run fast too. Here are six things you could learn to do. Think of at least one person who could teach you each new talent.

musician	swimmer	artist
chef	gardener	dancer

Think about a talent you have that you could teach someone else. Draw a picture of yourself doing this activity. Share it with a friend.

About the Author

Suzanne I. Barchers, Ed.D., began a career in writing and publishing after fifteen years as a teacher. She has written over 100 children's books, two college textbooks, and more than 20 reader's theater and teacher resource books. She previously held editorial roles at Weekly Reader and LeapFrog and is on the PBS Kids Media Advisory Board for the next generation of children's programming. Suzanne also plays the flute professionally—and for fun—from her home in Stanford, CA.

About the Illustrator

Mattia Cerato was born in Cuneo, a small town in northern Italy where he still lives and works. As soon as he could hold a pencil he loved sketching things he saw around him. When he is not drawing, Mattia loves traveling around the world, reading good books, and playing and listening to cool music.

 For a free activity page for this story, go to www.redchairpress.com and look for Free Activities.